The Mind of Wellonai

Prelude to The Shapewalker's Song

JH Tomen

For Karl

*et tui amóris in eis ignem accénde
renovábis fáciem terræ*

Kishtoran knelt in the sand, his palm flat against the earth as he listened to the stone. The apprentices he taught still needed to grit their teeth in concentration, but this had always come easily to him. It wasn't all natural talent, though. Most of it was just experience. The stone would speak when it wanted to. You couldn't rush it or force it. Some thought a talent for speaking to the wind meant they'd be able to do the rest, but wind spirits loved to gossip. That lack of patience was just another reason there were more itkousel than vikousel — let alone welkouyan like himself.

Still, it was good he had time to look around, because he needed to keep an eye on the ridgeline. There were things out here that would kill a man without breaking their stride, and if he died, it would be one less reader for his queen. Not to mention the shame he'd bring on his family… At least the view was soothing. It had been far too long since he'd been able to walk the spirit lands. The ridge was full of reds and golds, and the rock had been broken down by eons of wind, revealing the complex strata. Even down in the lowlands where they were, the sand was piled in beautiful waves, hillsides that melted into the nearly endless sky above.

Funny to think that some didn't find this landscape beautiful. He'd had to escort visitors here once with his father — some ocean-bound queen and her entourage, from where he couldn't remember — and he'd never forget what one of the foreign guards had said. A hard man with grey in his beard, his mouth had dropped open when they reached the edge of the spirit lands. "Nothing," the man had said in his thick accent, "so much…nothing." An ignorant thing to say, just revealing that the ocean-bound still had no idea of the value of these lands, though that was certainly for the best. Ever since the Berillai had built their train line in Kresonayun, it felt as though the prophesy was only growing closer. Even if they had only come to trade cattle like the rest of the ocean-bound, someday they'd realize the true value of these lands, and then all would be lost if he couldn't succeed in his work…

"Are you just going to stare at the sand all day, traitor?" the man behind Kishtoran asked. "Don't go thinking I'll deliver my side of the bargain if you don't deliver yours. No palladium means no path."

Kishtoran set his jaw, but sucked in a breath instead of speaking. An old trick of his father's for remaining calm. Everyone always seemed testier around a welkouyan — as if being hostile could negate how much more power they had than regular readers. "If men weren't fools," his father had liked to say, "no-one would have learned to hunt bears." Somehow, the trick still worked, and he found the venom gone from his tongue when he started to speak. Even the traitor bit no longer stung as much…

"These things take time, Enaroo," he said. "Just enjoy the view. I'll deliver my end."

"Fine," he grumbled, "just get on with it. I don't like the itrosen here. They're too excited."

Kishtoran paused, splitting his attention between the stone and the wind. The wind really *was* agitated. Perhaps Enaroo wasn't such a fool after all… The wind was always excitable, zipping to and fro, and it took a real reader to know when they were more excited than usual. For whatever reason, they loved to see activity in the spirit lands — fighting, hunting, dancing — it was all the same to them. But there shouldn't be any other humans for miles, so if the itrosen were getting excited...

He listened for another moment, but there was nothing specific in the wind chatter. He was thinking of asking the itrosen what they'd seen, but suddenly, he felt a tug from the earth. Just as he'd expected — the answer always came when you were paying the least attention. Not that a poraskun like Enaroo would understand that.

"I've got something," he said, closing his eyes so he could block out everything else.

"I knew you would!" Enaroo shouted happily, suddenly stepping up and slapping him on the back. Kishtoran swallowed his irritation, staying focused on that little tug from the earth. Losing it now would risk them wandering around the sands for another half day. Still, Enaroo was ignorant as ever, jabbering on.

"I told the others, traitor or not, it's not every day you have a welkouyan looking for work."

Kishtoran set his jaw again, but he didn't let go of that tiny thread from the earth. He pulled it, like silk, trying to find where the palladium was whispering to him. Still, Enaroo's comment nagged at him. Was he a traitor? *No!* He would never accept that about himself — he'd sooner die. Even if the bloody poraskuns were going to use the palladium to fight his own queen, what he was searching for would make all of that meaningless. Sometimes a man's loyalty must be to the divine — another saying of his father's. Kishtoran had already spent nearly half his life searching for this one clue, one measly step forward on the path his father had charted for him. If all he had to do was give up some palladium to his enemies, he would do it a hundred times over for the information he needed.

Finally, the thread he was pulling caught on something, like a fish catching on the end of a line. As Kishtoran began to pull — harder now, but still carefully as experience had taught him — the ground began to rumble. Even under ten feet of sand, the movement of the bedrock was enough to make the desert jump about. He could split the whole thing open, of course, but that would only be doing Enaroo a favor. The agreement was he'd find the palladium and bring up a nugget to prove it was there, not dig it up for him. Besides, the least he could do for his queen was buy her some time, forcing those poraskuns to dig around in the sand for a while before they could attack.

Kishtoran was still pulling, coaxing the palladium upwards when he suddenly heard a change in the wind. He opened his eyes just in time to see a hard gust of wind erupt over the next hillside, kicking up a cloud of sand. In the strange way of the spirit lands, the cloud seemed to coalesce again, like a wave cresting, and it swept down the hillside, blowing right towards them.

"I don't like the sound of that wind!" Enaroo shouted as the sand hit them. Kishtoran tried to keep his hold on the palladium, but he continued to stare out at the hill, squinting in the dust as he listened to the wind. Their whispering — or singing as some of the elders still liked to call it — had grown frantic. *Hunter,*

hunter, hunter, they seemed to chant giddily. Something was coming from over the ridgeline.

"We need to go, traitor!" Enaroo continued yelling over the rush of the wind. "You can get your path tomorrow. Morning is always safer anyway."

"I'm not turning back now," Kishtoran said, gritting his teeth as he focused all his energy on the ground again. As if this poraskun would show him the path after he knew where the bloody palladium was! He'd weasel off to his people and tell them the location so they could come back in the night. And even if a welkouyan could destroy both the palladium and the diggers in a single blow, they both knew Kishtoran wouldn't be able to sit in the spirit lands night and day waiting for them.

Finally, the thread went slack as a nugget of palladium released itself from the stone. He was nearly there! He just needed to pull it up to the surface. The rumbling of the ground picked up as he painstakingly urged the bedrock to shift its form to create a path. The rock still didn't want to hurry, though, at least once it was rumbling it was easier to coax. Kishtoran only had a mind for the stone now, as if they had become one, dancing together as they eased the palladium towards the surface. But suddenly, the rumbling of the earth seemed to heighten, far more than it should have from his actions alone.

"Oh Sacred Mother of the Sands," Enaroo muttered behind him, "it's nearly here. It must be a whole pack of hunters."

Kishtoran gritted his teeth again, trying to force the stone to hurry. The palladium was only ten feet beneath the surface now. He wouldn't be both a traitor and a failure!

"Come on you idiot," Enaroo hissed, no longer feeling safe enough to shout, but his urgency as strong as a scream. "You know once they see us there's no escaping."

"Run then," Kishtoran spat out, but Enaroo didn't move. He likely knew he'd be better off with a welkouyan, even if the hunters would rip them both to shreds without a second thought. And based on the rumbling, they were probably dealing with kerosemal…not something you even wanted to have a nightmare about.

The rumbling grew more intense from beyond the hillside,

the heavy pounding of kerosemal at a run. Kishtoran closed his eyes again. Even with hunters coming across the sand, he couldn't afford to lose his bond with the stone. The rock was finally trusting him, and he'd lose everything if he gave up now and had to start over. Especially once a nugget had been released from a vein of palladium, the metal was likely to get crushed if the earth decided to swallow back the borehole he was creating. But there clearly wasn't time, either. Enaroo began to blubber behind him, weeping as he froze to the sand.

Come! he shouted in his mind to the rock. The shaking hit a crescendo, his arm beginning to wobble where it met the ground. He heard a terrible screech from over the hillside, the hunter having picked up their smell. Kishtoran pulled with all his might, and the ground finally split, the nugget of palladium shooting up like one of those ocean-bound cannon balls, spinning into the air as it ripped through the sand. Kishtoran leapt up from his knee, snatching the palladium as he spun back to Enaroo. The man had fallen over and was sprawled out on the ground, as if he could hide himself in the sand. Kishtoran slid along the ground to him, grabbing his back and pulling the man into an embrace as they both began to glow with a golden light.

Not a moment later, the two men were gone, a yeko tree in their place as the glowing light subsided. Kishtoran could still feel Enaroo's blubbering inside the tree, but he ignored it, trying to maintain his calm as he reached out with his mind. Even a tree could see the world in a way. It was like reading the wind — as the tree touched the air around it, it could form a hazy sense of its surroundings. He stretched that vision as far as it could go, to a distance only a welkouyan could achieve, encompassing the entire valley and the ridgeline. As his awareness met the colorful stone of the hillside, he felt his spirit freeze as he took in the awful form of the kerosemal.

He didn't fear them as others did — they were holy, after all, protecting the spirit lands for the Mother of the Sands — though it was impossible not to lose some part of your nerve when you finally saw one. It was the length of one of those strange train cars the ocean-bound had designed and just as wide. Its head was flat, like a snake's, though it had seven eyes perched all around its head. They said kerosemal could even hunt birds in the sky using their seventh eye, which faced straight up. It had its long tail lifted into the air, trying to smell them, and its ten legs seemed to bore into the rock. Kishtoran felt Enaroo's spirit tremble as the kerosemal let out another piercing cry, the others in its pack answering from somewhere behind it.

He felt one of those giant eyes focus on them, and Kishtoran focused on being absolutely still — not that a tree could move much. Even so, stone reading wasn't something you did lightly in the spirit lands, and the kerosemal would be skeptical. They had minds as powerful as a man's in his estimation — just another benefit of their closeness with the Sacred Mother. While it waited to hear from the others in its pack, it would surely be wondering if they really were a tree. He'd watched them hunt once with his father — from the safety of a faraway cliff. They'd seemed to swim in the sand, their long legs piercing through the desert until they met the bedrock, only the tops of their heads and the ends of the tails sticking out as they fanned into a giant triangle, the pack covering more ground in a minute than a man could run in a week.

Finally, after what seemed to be a year, another piercing cry sounded from far off, and the kerosemal cocked its head, answering the call before turning away from their valley. Kishtoran still waited a long while, until the rumbling of the ground was gone and the itrosen went back to their normal empty chatter. Then he released Enaroo, the golden light returning until they both stood there again, two separate men on the sand.

"You bloody poraskun!" Enaroo shouted, pacing along the sand with his hands yanking on his hair. Enaroo was a hulking man —probably a tavern brawler in another life — and looked like he might be tempted to take a swing at him if he hadn't been afraid to hit a welkouyan. "You could've had us killed," Enaroo continued, "and you wouldn't even care. Over nothing but a fairy tale, as if the bloody Mind of Wellonai is even real! I was fine to let you wander the desert until you withered to dust, but not if you're going to drag me along with—"

"Enaroo," Kishtoran said sharply, making the man stop his pacing. He opened his palm, showing him the perfectly round nugget of palladium. It was the size of a large egg, and it glittered a beautiful bronzish silver in the sunlight. Enaroo's mouth fell open and he stepped towards him with an outstretched hand.

"Not yet," Kishtoran said, closing his hand. "You're going to show me that path, or I'll march you back here and make you watch me destroy the entire vein."

Enaroo shook his head, coming out of the trance the palladium had put him in.

"Fine," he said, skulking back towards where they'd left their packs. "It's only a few more hours from here. I brought you the map like you said. But after that, we're done. I don't ever want to see your face again. Understand, traitor?"

"Sure, I understand," Kishtoran said, grinning. The man could call him whatever he liked now. Once he found the Mind of Wellonai, there would be nothing to stop the prophesy and all would be forgiven.

——————————) ——————————

Queen Minara ni So'kenaliyan, Queen of the Pentine Clan,
Daughter of the Snake River and Keeper of the Red Lands,
looked at herself in a mirror, appraising the makeup her servants
had applied in her tent that morning. She still had some traces of
circles under her eyes, though there was little her servants could
do about that without covering her in so much paste that she'd
look like one of those masked fools in C'erinalay. Still, she
smiled. She may not look her best — there was too much to lose
sleep over these days for that — but at least she was herself.

We would look better in the white robe, her other half
thought, already sounding testy despite the sun barely being
above the ridge.

"No," she said firmly to herself in the mirror. "The moon is
half over the Serin Valley, and that means it's my turn to rule. I
forbid you to question anything this day, especially what I wear."

There was no answer to that, though she did feel her chest
flush with heat. So be it; she would not let anything ruin this
week. The ocean-bound were coming for a celebration to

commemorate their final train line. Like all ocean-bound, they had likely only agreed to it to show off their soldiers and puff their chests, but this was truly her day of victory. Even with threats on all sides, she had worked too long and hard not to celebrate this success. It had taken every ounce of her cunning to have this station built in the Red Lands, and this would ensure that it was *her* people who fulfilled the prophecy.

That was, if she could find her welkouyan before the rest of her plans crumbled to dust… Kishtoran had been missing for over a week, and not a single one of the vikousel apprentices he trained so closely would give her a single peep as to where he'd gone. Her heart fluttered a bit at the thought of him, but she gritted her teeth and shut out the thought. It was not *her* half of her mind who was in love with that silly poraskun, and she wouldn't waste her energy on such foolish thoughts — not today! She just wanted him back before any of the other clans knew he was missing. Speaking of which, she'd need one of her esskousel to take his form during the ceremonies before someone noted his absence…

She rang her bell, summoning her maid as she pushed herself up from the mirror table. There was too much to be done not to begin the day at once. She walked over to the side of her bed to choose a crown. Even in the darkness of the tent where she was only lit by a single mirrored lamp, four of the five crowns shone as their metal picked up the light. Still, she didn't pick up any of the gilded things. Instead, she picked up her mother's crown, the one that had passed down in her family since the beginning of time, when the true children were born in the sands of the spirit lands. The others were just trophies, seized from the other clans that made up the entirety of her people now. They too were older than most memories, but they could still be counted with years, and they would not do for such an important week.

She reached out, gently taking her mother's crown and placing it on her head. By contrast, it had no gilding to speak of. It was a perfect circle of finely polished yeko wood, the only ornamentation in the form of an equally perfect circle of palladium in the center. This, she arranged directly over her forehead. She could already feel herself becoming more alert, the wisdom of her ancestors lifting her as it poured into her mind from the coronet.

Be with me today, mother, she thought, this time thinking with her own mind. There were days when your parents walked behind your shoulder, even if they had left forever for the spirit lands. She gritted her teeth again — that was another favorite saying of Kishtoran's, that fool poraskun! Luckily, her maid arrived at that moment, pulling open the tent flap and banishing all her foolish thoughts with the morning light.

"My lady, Daughter of the Timeless Sand," the old woman said formally, bowing low despite her years. Feras had tended her since she was a child, yet she still insisted on the proper titles. Her father had been a stickler, so the habit would surely die hard, even if she herself was decidedly not. Still, it seemed to please Feras to think of herself as the lady's maid to the daughter of the timeless sand, so she allowed it.

"How may I serve?" Feras asked, returning to standing. At least her posture was not overly formal after bowing. The old woman also smiled when she saw the coronet — a beautiful smile, and one that made her look almost young again. Her mother had always cared deeply for Feras, and there was a loyalty there that simply could not be bought. It was certainly more than she could ever hope for from her official advisors.

"I need Sorenin brought to me at once," Minara said, picking the only esskousel Feras could summon without notifying anyone else. A sudden look of fear came over Feras's face, but she blinked it away. Minara could hardly blame her — Sorenin was her only son, after all.

"Nothing dangerous," Minara added quickly. "It would just be better if no-one knew what work I was about this week with the Berillai. Have him come in the private way."

"Right away, my lady," Feras said, the smile returning to her face. She had been the one to think up the scheme for privately accessing Minara's chambers, and that seemed to wipe away any remaining nervousness she felt for her son. "I will have the tea service here for you shortly."

With another round of bowing, Feras backed out of the sleeping tent, and Minara followed her out into the anteroom. It was some thirty feet long and connected her three private tents for dining, bathing, and sleeping. The front panels had been removed as they were every morning, and light poured in from the desert. Already, three of her ministers were waiting by the water basin in the center of the tent, sipping the mineral water from the golden cups there for the purpose. Minara frowned. The ministers were allowed the water by the rights of their station, of course, but she was running fearfully low on the stuff. If Kishtoran didn't return soon, she'd have to have one of the vikousel find a new aquifer for her, and who knew if they'd be able to find the kind she liked…

"Brothers," Minara said, inclining her head as the men looked up. They'd likely thought the rustle of her tent flap was just the maid leaving, but to their credit, they all scrambled to put down their chalices and bow.

"My Sister of the Sands," Jerobis said, stepping forward out of his bow and taking her hand to kiss. Part of her filled with revulsion as the slimy man put his lips to her palm, but Minara shrugged off the feeling. It was the other part of herself who despised the man — something to do with watching him devour a sausage at a high feast — but her own memories of the event were muddled at best. More important to her own plans, the man spoke Berillai fluently, and he had been essential in completing the treaty for the train station. The two halves of her mind were agreed on those plans in the abstract, of course, but she had always been the one with the sense if not the passion.

"The Berillai are nearly here," Jerobis said, smiling widely beneath his thick braided mustache. "They had to stop the train for repairs in Kerosim, but our riders saw them and sent a hawk. They should be here within the hour."

"Excellent," Minara said, inclining her head again, just managing to maintain her queenly calm as she fought the urge to gulp. So close already? She had dealt with the Berillai before, of course, but they were sending some general to commemorate the signing of the treaty, along with as many soldiers as they could fit onto that metal beast they called a train. She wasn't afraid, just…apprehensive. The Berillai had a fearsome reputation — enough so to make her grateful every day that the Relimorans had refused any part of the Four Nations war between the ocean-bound — but mostly, they were just odd. Their accents were strange, they seldom laughed, and they didn't even believe in the child gods the way the other ocean-bound did. Some said they worshipped the ocean itself, which didn't seem to fit at all. How did they find the nerve to step upon the Sacred Mother's back without the proper forms of worship?

"You two," she said to the other ministers, "do you have anything to report?"

The other two men, Jerobis's underlings, looked at each other. Bad news, then. The two usually tripped over each other to report the good news, and for some reason feared her wrath with the bad. She thought herself fairly reasonable, though, of course, she couldn't be in control all the time… Still, it could also be Jerobis they feared. Compared to their boss — who was built like a fire kettle — the underlings were shaped like those strange bean stalks the Secharin grew by the southern river. At any rate, it wasn't as if they were responsible for the bad news, though her people could be admittedly skittish about omens, even more so than the rest of the True Clans.

"Well," began the man on the left, Teroshi, "the cattle thefts seem to have continued."

Minara nodded. The man had spoken too quickly, volunteering the cattle thefts. Besides, that was nothing new these past few months, which must mean there was something even worse to report…

"How many this time?" she asked.

"Two dozen," Teroshi said with a grimace. "It seems the headmaster was away — coming for the festival with the Berillai, I think — and they killed his apprentice in the night."

"Where?" Minara asked, her throat growing tight. The cattle thefts were becoming more commonplace, true, but this was the first time blood had been shed. Surely it was only a matter of time if the herdsmen were keeping a closer guard, but this was certainly brazen.

"North of the Snake River," Teroshi said, "by the Seven Dunes."

Minara bit her lip. That was awfully close to Kikaso Clan

lands. They'd made their opposition to the train line more than clear, and that was also unfortunately the last place Kishtoran had been seen. Her heart threatened to do a somersault just thinking his name, but she kept the reins tight on that part of her mind. There was far more to worry about than that lout.

"And you?" she said to Ressoib, the other minister. "What bad omens do you have for me?" The man's eyes widened and he began to stammer, but she cut him off. "On second thought," she said, turning to Jerobis, "you can tell me yourself."

The man blinked, but at least kept his bearings — more so than his underlings, anyway.

"There's talk of caravans on the move — Kikaso by the sound of it — heading towards the spirit lands. A good two hundred of them left before dawn. One of our scouts was searching for the cattle thief and picked up their trail."

Very bad indeed. Her mind began to race, trying to put the pieces together. Ruling was like the games she'd played as a girl where you had to move the beads through a tangle of string to the other side, only ten times more knotted. First Kishtoran, then the cattle and those cursed Kikaso poraskuns inexplicably leaving camp. And all of it the week the Berillai arrived… No queen believed in coincidence, and her least of all. She needed time to think. How to keep a hold on the treaty signing without letting her guard down? She was about to open her mouth when Feras returned, turning the corner into the tent at a dash with a tea basket in her hands. Right on time.

"I must ask you to leave me, brothers," she said to the ministers. "Continue the preparations for the banquets; I will decide how to handle the cattle thieves. For now, though, I must think. Just send me the Spearmaster whenever you're able."

The three men all muttered several titles as they bowed their way out of the tent. As soon as they were out of sight, Minara clapped her hands together.

"Excellent work, Feras," she said, ushering the woman through to the dining tent. The woman looked near to fainting with happiness as she hurried through with the tea basket. Perhaps she needed to be more sparing with her praise of the woman… For once, the old woman hadn't even noticed that

Minara had broken protocol by holding the tent flap open for her.

The dining tent was large enough to hold a dozen clan chiefs when required, but at the moment, it was only set up for herself, the servants usually changing the furniture over in the night while she slept so it would be ready for her breakfast. As it was, there was a low kesok table inlaid with ivory and a single gold-threaded pillow beside it. Apparently coming back to her senses, Feras stood just behind the pillow as she waited for Minara to sit, though she still shuffled her feet as if she were apt to start dancing the susr'enah.

Once she'd primly folded her legs under her on the pillow, Feras pulled the top off the basket, slinging the wicker straps behind her back as she began emptying the contents. There was her usual silver-worked teapot and her favorite cup and honey bowl. At the end, however, Feras put down an extra cup, this one made of clay with a tight-fitting lid. Feras nodded towards the mug, smiling as she moved to pour the tea. Minara removed the lid, revealing a large scarab beetle that occupied nearly the entire thing.

She started, nearly dropping the lid. She'd known Sorenin would be arriving in the tea basket, of course, though she'd been startled by the beetle all the same. Sorenin was a mischievous one… Couldn't he have come as a ladybug or something? His mother must have let slip how much she loathed the disgusting creatures. She clicked her tongue, picking up the cup with just two fingers.

"On with it then!" she said, shaking the cup. The beetle opened its shell, buzzing across the tent with its ghastly wings until it set down just beyond the tea table. Then it glowed with a golden light, revealing the form of Sorenin.

"My Lady of the Sands," he said, nodding. He was far less formal than his mother, thankfully, though most of the guards were. Even with his eyes right on her, though, the man felt aloof somehow. He never said much, and he would take time to respond to questions, but he was a good bodyguard all the same. It was just her own pet theory, but it must have something to do with being esskousel. They always seemed to be the dreamiest of the true children. Vikousel were reserved, true, but there was a hardness to them, while the itkousel may as well be as flighty as the wind itself.

She supposed the esskousel must have their reasons — she certainly did — though it did make her wonder. She was like their cousin, in her own way, but she had to deal with having her mind cleft in two. What was their excuse? There was a rumbling from the other half of her at that, as if thinking about their way of life invited her into the conversation, but that was a distraction she could not afford. Minara shook her head, focusing back on Sorenin.

"Kishtoran is missing," she said — she may as well get to the truth of it if he was to serve her in this role. "It seems things are coming to a head with our enemies, but it is crucial that his absence go unnoticed while the Berillai are here. Do you know his form?"

Sorenin blinked, but then nodded. He closed his eyes for the briefest moment before glowing again, appearing in the form of her welkouyan, that foolish coat of his included.

"Good," she said, "let's begin."

Kishtoran moved through the sand as lightly as he could, his eyes half closed as he focused trance-like on the stone beneath him. It had been five days of wandering already, the landscape around him just as unchanged and eternal as when he'd begun. Still, this was the work he had trained his entire life for, and he would see it through. Even if it meant some other poor soul found his bones generations from now, he would press on.

At least the map that poraskun Enaroo had given him was real. That had governed his first three days, getting him past the Iron Fingers and the Death Lake. The rest of the journey, however, he would have to chart himself. The stone he was following held a tiny trace of palladium, running like a thin river deeper and deeper into the spirit lands. Still, it was barely noticeable, hardly even a glimmer now, and it took every ounce of his focus not to lose it. He supposed he should see a blessing in that, because even finding it in the first place as he left the path seemed like a miracle.

Like all of the true clans, Enaroo's had maintained their own path through the spirit lands. The paths took generations to build, and they were sacred things, each one built step by brutal step in an attempt to fulfill the prophesy. Even if they denied it, every true Relimoran prayed it would be their destiny to fulfill it, hoping beyond hope that their own people would be the ones to return in glory to the kingdom of the gods.

Secret paths or not, though, finding the Mind of Wellonai was no easy task, of course. The Relimorans kept the oldest calendars on Wellonai — far older than those fool "histories" of the ocean-bound — and even so, they'd been searching for over a thousand years. Perhaps it really was a sacrilege to hope so fervently for something the goddess herself didn't even seem to desire. Wellonai had died coming to this world, after all, and if she wanted to be made whole, why had she split herself into three? He supposed the child gods were still alive — the ocean-bound worshipped them, at any rate — but they were only her blood, her voice, and her breath. It was Wellonai's Mind that had given men the ability to think, given the wind the ability to whisper. If they weren't meant to seek out the Holy Mother of the Sands and make her whole, then why give them minds in the first place? Why not make them like the cattle that covered Relimora like so many grains of sand?

Whatever the answers to those questions, he was no heretic. More than anyone he had ever met — besides his father, of course — he lived and breathed the search for Wellonai. Some of the clans claimed the spirit lands were a barrier to keep men out, of course — though even those clans maintained paths, even if they insisted they were just for the rituals. He preferred his father's interpretation. If the spirit lands were a barrier, it was only to the unworthy. To the holy, it was simply a challenge. The one who finally found such a relic, who sacrificed everything for its sake, would be the one the Mother would trust to resurrect her.

It was that conviction that had brought him this far. The belief he could swallow any amount of sorrow if it saw Wellonai made whole — even being labeled a traitor or dealing with those damned poraskuns. It was conviction that had kept him following his father on so many trips into these lands, kept him training with stones until his fingers bled, driving him to become a full welkouyan. And it was conviction that had kept him traveling secretly between the clans since his father died, that gave him the strength to read scrolls late into the night until his eyes grew bleary. It was conviction that had given him this clue, that single godly thread that had led him to the Kikaso.

All of the clans believed their path was the true path, of course. And in a place so vast and desolate, each one had merit. They had all been charted by vikousel and welkouyan over centuries, finding the routes through the desert that would avoid the giant chasms that could swallow armies in the dunes, weaving their way between the tiny oases that could keep you alive once your canteen was empty. Still, all paths ended at some point, waiting for some other fool to take it up, daring to hope they'd reach their true destination. This path, though…this path *was* different, it had to be.

Kishtoran slowed for a moment, the coins in his cheeks telling him he needed water — another old trick of his father's. If you were going to survive in these lands, you needed to know when to drink and when to wait. Any fool could tell his mouth was dry in the sands, but if you drank your water all at once you would never have enough to make the return, the oases lay too far apart to save you from your own foolishness. So he always marched with a coin on either side of his mouth, one copper and one silver. The copper you could taste all the time, the sharp tang ever present. Silver, however, was far more subtle, and only when your mouth was at its driest could you sense the strange sweetness over the taste of the copper.

He stopped, breaking himself from his meditations and looking at the desert around him. He kept a fraction of his mind on the palladium, of course, but in all honesty, it came as a shock to take in his surroundings after so long in the marcher's trance. He took his pack off and set it to the side, rolling his shoulders. His water skin was about half empty already, so he'd need to look for water here, scant as it would be. There had been a good oasis near the end of the poraskun's trail where he'd been able to refill, but there was no promise he'd find another one. Besides, he didn't even know where he was going anymore beyond following this strip of palladium.

He took a deep breath, easing himself onto the sand and crossing his legs. When looking for something as large as the palladium vein with Enaroo, it had been simple enough to just kneel with a palm on the ground, but searching for water this deep in the spirit lands was a different matter entirely. He would need a far deeper connection to the stones if he was going to nudge them into revealing something so precious as water. First, though, he ought to ask the wind. As much of a waste of time it would be out here, the itrosen at least didn't guard their secrets closely.

Kishtoran shifted his awareness towards the air around him, feeling the desert wind whipping past him over the dunes. He aligned himself to its flow, rocking slowly back and forth in the direction the wind was heading. Itrosen didn't like to slow down for long, and they'd only think you a fool if you sat like a stone on the ground. Then, he began to breathe out, matching his breath to the whirring voice of the wind that filled his ears as it rushed past.

Pesokunarayan, he thought in the language of the gods. An image appeared in his mind, a large pool of water, lapping against the sides of a shallow stone crevice where it had pooled up. He kept his mind on that pool, repeating the word in his mind as the wind continued past him, allowing the thought to pass from his mind into the mind of the wind. As the wind picked up on what he was thinking, they began to chatter in his mind, like the chirps of birds surrounding him on all sides.

Water, water, water, a thousand itrosen seemed to say in unison, almost like children all laughing at the same joke.

No, no, no, they began to answer as the request stretched along the length of the river of wind coming over the dunes. Some of the more helpful ones among them at least put images into his mind of where they'd last seen water. Unfortunately, he recognized it immediately as the poraskun oasis he'd left behind days ago.

"Fair enough," he said to himself, opening his eyes and banishing the wind from his mind. Then he rolled up his sleeves, baring the full length of his arm before leaning forward until his forehead touched the ground. He breathed into the pose, letting his arms sink into the sand as his palms pressed into the earth. He waited for a long while, focusing on his breath, until he finally found the voice of the earth. It could be jarring after the itrosen, their thousands of chirps fading away to the single voice of the stone.

Vitrosen weren't actually singular, of course, but they were so massive that it was hard to tell the difference. He imagined them to be like those strange drawings of whales he'd seen in ocean-bound books — massive creatures drifting beneath the surface. A single stone spirit could stretch for miles, huge swaths of bedrock caught up in its sliver of mind. That scale, however, was part of what made seeking them out so different. Getting them to notice you was like waking a karu bull in winter — you had to find them in the depths, where the true spirit of the rock lay hidden somewhere at the base of the land.

Instead of swaying as he had with the wind, Kishtoran became absolutely still. He was tempted to even take the shape of a stone, but for now, he focused solely on the ways of the vikousel. When he felt as if his very blood had stopped flowing, he pushed out with his mind, sounding for the stone.

Pesokunarayan, he thought again, letting the word seep from his body into the sand. He continued that way for a time, thinking the sacred word over and over, but slowly and steadily, like striking a giant drum that took ten men to move.

Finally, he felt a response. Not an answer, not yet, but a sort of echo, like his voice had finally bounced off something, the giant rolling over in its slumber. It seemed he had his vitrosen. Now that he could feel where it was, it was easier to direct his voice towards it. It was somewhere to the east and perhaps a mile deep if his judgment wasn't off. It seemed to be the god of the next mountain ridge, its back easily extending ten miles in either direction. That was a relief — he'd been hoping for a large one. If anyone knew where water would be this far into the spirit lands, she ought to. For all their stillness, it was the memories of the vitrosen that were so powerful. Itrosen could remember what they'd seen an hour ago, but they knew about as much of the land as a human did. The stones, on the other hand, saw time like a horizon, something they could pick from at their will.

Pessssssoooookuuuuunaaaaraaaayaaaaaan, the vitrosen finally replied in its low quaking voice. It sounded like limestone. His father had taught him to recognize their families, though why the slabs varied out here in the spirit lands was beyond him. The land began to shift, the hillside shaking slowly back and forth beneath him. He stayed absolutely still, ready to absorb whatever the stone chose to tell. Eventually, the moving earth began to take on a true rhythm, and images entered his mind, the voice of the earth starting to align with the rhythms of his own body.

He saw this place, the dunes shifting quickly, moving under the force of the winds, growing and shrinking under a thousand different skies. It took only moments, but in the way of the stone memories, he was surely seeing thousands of years pass by in an eye blink. He began to see days of rain, truly precious events in the spirit lands. He could remember maybe three in his lifetime, though the vitrosen could remember hundreds. More importantly, she remembered where the water went, sending him images of it running down the dunes, pooling in the lowlands, the feel of it on her back when it broke through the sands and touched stone. She always lapped it up then, capturing it and burying it deep within the rock.

While he kept his mind on that image of the water soaking into the stone, he thought his name to the vitrosen. *Kishtoran*, he thought slowly, in the same measured drum beats from before. Like all names, it was a sacred thing, embodying a meaning that only Wellonai truly knew. Still, the stone would know his meaning. Could the water be given to one such as him? A humble human spirit that had no sense of time. He would drink up in moments the water that had taken her centuries to collect.

Sheeeeetaaaaarrrraaaayaaaallll, she finally responded.

Thank you, he thought in his own tongue, *thank you for sparing me*. The ground began to shake to a different rhythm, the stone moving more assertively than before, though it was gentler than when he'd taken the palladium. All spirits seemed to know that water was a sacred, fragile thing, and one deserving of care. Metal could be shot out of the stone like one of those ocean-bound cannons, but water would dissipate in these lands faster than the snap of your fingers.

Finally, he heard a cracking sound, the stone just beneath him splitting. He gently lifted himself up, carefully scooping away the sand with his hands. Luckily, the sand wasn't deep here at the top of the dune, the wind pushing it down the banks every time it piled up. Eventually, he revealed a narrow fissure in the bedrock, about the width of his hand. Water was pooling up there, filling it like a bowl as the stone spirit sent it to him drop by painstaking drop.

He waited for it to fill, but then he didn't dare wait any longer. The vitrosen would know how much water she had, and once the bowl was filled, there would be no more. He dunked his hand into the pool, wanting to laugh at how good the coolness felt under the sun. He scooped it up and sat back on his heels, gratefully tipping the water into his mouth. It took time to drink it by the handful, but it was the only way. Putting anything but his skin into her pool would disgrace her. Still, it only made the water taste better, and he took it bit by bit until it was gone.

When he was finished, he put his forehead on the stone again, just to the side of the fissure, and gave his thanks. Then he stood, feeling like a new man, as if he had been born from that fissure instead of the water. He laughed in spite of himself, running his hands through is hair as he tilted his head back, closing his eyes in the sun. He'd never found so much water, and he'd certainly never expected this much so far in the spirit lands.

Finding water always made him wonder, though. Where did the rains come from? Storm clouds from the sea would never make it this far, and the spirit lands themselves were said to stretch farther than the lifetime of a man could span. And what of the oases? Even though he couldn't speak to them — not even a welkouyan could speak to all things — he could still tell that they had spirits. Somehow there were slivers of mind there, collecting water from the depths and bringing it to the surface. But where did that water come from? That made him think of the poraskun song, of course. There had to be some answers in it about this place, though he still hadn't been able to puzzle the whole thing out. That was what had brought him here, after all, and the man who'd written it must have known far more about the spirit lands than he could ever hope to.

Kishtoran picked up his pack and began to walk again. There was no telling how much further he had to go, but he just had to focus on reaching the next ridgeline, and then the one after that. He hummed as he walked now, trying to summon the lyrics of the song. He had only seen the words written down, so he didn't know what the actual music was meant to be, but it was easier to remember things with a tune, so he had set it to one of his mother's lullabies.

The vein of truth, it stretched so true, throughout the sea of sand.

I reached the second bowl of life, its water in my hand.

The spirit told me many things, its truths that spanned all time,

It sent me to the east again, the secrets there sublime.

There's still no way I can survive, I'll never see my home.

But I send this song of wind to you, these secrets you might know.

From afar I saw a mount of stone, its hue the truest green.

Follow me into the sands, and you'll know what I mean.

That song had been passed down for generations by those poraskun Kikaso, though they'd apparently only thought it another traveler's song. Not him, though. The moment he found it in the library at Serikat, he'd fallen to his knees, realizing what it must be. Someone had seen a glimpse of the Mind of Wellonai, though they hadn't been able to survive the return. The poraskuns had a legend about that song. They said a spirit walker who had died had sent it to them, using his last breath to sing it to the wind, his own legs unable to carry him back through the sands. He'd known then he'd finally found the clue he'd been missing. He'd known he had to find the poraskun map and trace the vein of palladium towards whatever "green mount" that man had found. It was there he would find the Mind of Wellonai.

Kishtoran finally came over the ridgeline, the dune sweeping down into a valley that seemed to stretch to infinity. He paused, leaning over with his hands on his knees for a moment. After he caught his breath, he stood, scanning the horizon. He was reaching out for the palladium again when he caught sight of something in the distance. A good few miles off, in the center of the valley, was what looked to be a mountain, but one made up of hundreds of sharp crags. And in the center… Kishtoran's mouth fell open and he dropped to his knees. The center of the mountain was the brightest green he had ever seen, an emerald peeking out from the sands.

"Thank you," he whispered, feeling a tear come to his eye. Had he had such little faith in himself? In the prophesy? It was shocking to realize, but it was true. Even risking everything for this, a part of him had believed he'd find nothing. He went down to his hands and knees, leaning his face to the ground where he kissed the sands. It was all he could do for Wellonai, the sacred mother of all things, the giver of life, the creator of minds. Even his thank you seemed so pitiful, but what could ever match the goddess of truth?

Somehow, he finally felt his strength return, and he leaned back on his heels, laughter suddenly bubbling up in him as he wiped the tears and sand from his face. He sniffed, still laughing as he looked up at the sky.

"*Kishtoralenam,* Papa," he whispered. That had been his father's favorite word in the language of the gods — "we go together", it was said to mean. It almost made him laugh harder — talking to the sky like some poraskun! Why did they talk to the sky when they sought the dead if their spirits were held in the earth with Wellonai? Perhaps the stone was too sleepy, too ancient to care for their petty whispers. Perhaps only the wind would carry such a message to the world beneath. Whatever it was, it didn't matter. All he hoped was that wherever he was, his father could hear. His father had set him on this path, and his father's hand had guided him to this moment, the moment for all their people when the prophesy would be revealed at last.

He finally stood, shaking his head as he found his balance again. Still smiling, he shifted his pack on his shoulders and started for the edge of the dune. It would be a while yet to cross that much sand, and the sun didn't have as much left to its arc as he'd like. He took his first step, reaching the edge of the hill when he froze again, this time the smile vanishing from his face.

Keroooooowa, came the call, the blood-curdling cry of kerosemal. Kishtoran froze, straining his ears. It was distant, right? It couldn't be for him. Besides, their cries could travel for miles in the emptiness of the spirit lands.

Keroooooowa, he heard again, closer this time. There were no coincidences in a place this desolate. Here, at the heart of the spirit lands, there was no doubt the hunters had come for him. Kishtoran ran, launching himself over the hills and down the dunes.

Minara held out her arm, her muscles burning under the weight of the heavy glass, but the plastered smile never left her face. The Berillai minister continued to drone on, their fifth toast in a row, all of it washed down by this awful ale they had brought by the crate on their poraskun train. She could hardly complain — drinking with a bunch of ocean-bound was a small price to pay for the future of your people, of all peoples, really — but she longed for a glass of sekka wine all the same. There was no subtlety to this ale, no sweetness, nothing that could be called flavor.

It fit the Berillai, she supposed. Sekka trees took a generation to bloom; they required patience and skill to tend at the edge of the desert. The Berillai ale, on the other hand, was just hard grain, forced to grow in a single season from lands that held snow — snow! Was that why they were so impatient? Whatever the reason, it did make her wonder… How exactly was the sky supposed to drop solid rain? The spirit lands were dangerously cold at night, but cold came from the lack of water, not the abundance of it.

"— and we shall never forget this future of prosperity to which we are all committed," the Berillai minister said, finally finishing as he raised his glass.

"Hear, hear!" the others yelled, raising their glasses even higher. Minara did the same, forcing herself to choke down the vile stuff, the smile never leaving her face by even a hair. At least this was the last night of their state visit. Soon, the treaty would be signed, and they'd return on that awful train, belching smoke back to their own ocean-bound lands.

I should lead, the other half of her mind tittered at her. *You know I don't grimace from a little ale.*

Minara squeeze her eyes shut tight for a moment, using the last second of drinking to hide her face. *No!* she thought sharply. The barrier between her minds was slipping with the alcohol, but it was still her turn to lead. Besides, they needed subtlety for a state dinner, not the raucous fearlessness of her other half. The way she drank in those times…it made her shudder to remember. But even for the savage Berillai, that kind of drinking was better off at a battle feast than the signing of a treaty.

She lowered her glass, resuming her graceful smile as the Berillai minister made eye contact with her.

"My lady, Minara," he said, nodding, still using the bare minimum of titles — as if they were equals! — "perhaps you'd like to say a few words."

"Yes," she said, inclining her head. It was an effort to stand gracefully from the strange chairs the Berillai had brought — she felt all knees without the soft base of a pillow to stand from — but she managed somehow, smoothing her dress as she took up her own glass again.

"My dear friends," she said, "on behalf of all the people of the Pentine Clan, I wish to—" An ear-splitting blast seemed to tear the air apart, shaking the ground and throwing her from her feet. Kishtoran — no, Sorenin — was there in a flash, taking her by the elbow and lifting her up. Her ears were ringing, but she kept her feet, nodding to Sorenin before gently stepping free of his support. The Berillai delegation was in equal disarray, cups of ale spilled everywhere and half the men standing from their chairs, looking as if they were struggling to choose between running away and drawing their swords.

"What happened?" she asked the minister, her eyes darting around. "Is it possible your train—"

"That's no train, my lady," he said, coming up to her. "They run on steam and the boiler's been off for hours. Someone must be trying to upend our talks. Guards," he said, turning to his men, "prepare for—"

Just then, the head of the city's wall guard, Seruva, came running into the tent, a wild look in her eyes.

"My Queen," she said, "we're under attack. Archers on the western ridge, Kikaso I think. But they…they're hitting us with something strange, they've already breached one part of the wall."

"The wall?" Minara asked. "Impossible, the spirits—"

"There's something on the arrows," Seruva said. "Terosin said the walls aren't responding to him at the site of the explosion."

Another round of explosions sounded, from somewhere to

the south. They were further from the tent this time, but they still seemed to make the air crackle. Minara felt a tug on her mind, the other half of her trying to seize control. Minara, shook her head, fighting her off as she clamped her eyes closed.

I need to lead, the other half said. *This is no longer diplomacy, this is war!*

No! Minara snapped. *We can salvage this*. But when she opened her eyes, she caught the look on the Berillai minister's face. A desperate look. Forget the accord, a man like that could easily cut a hole through her own people in an attempt to escape.

Fine, she thought. *Save us*. She felt herself drift away, floating to the back of her mind as she gave up control of her body.

"Kishtoran," Minarin said, turning to her guard. "Rally all the vikousel, we have to protect the walls." Seronin nodded once, flashing with golden light into a pigeon. He soared from the tent, off to find whoever he could to speak to the walls. "And Minister," she said turning to the Berillai man. His eyes had doubled in size at the esskousel transforming, but that was no longer her concern. "I'll double your annual cattle tribute if you help save my city." The man nodded, apparently unable to speak.

"Good," she said, turning back to Seruva as the ground shook again. "We fight."

Kishtoran slid down the dunes, his heart racing. He skidded to a stop at the bottom before getting up at a sprint. His feet pounded on the stone — somehow there was no sand surrounding that strange green mountain — his arms pumping and his lungs burning. He dropped his pack, anything to make him faster, though it probably wouldn't be enough. The kerosemal had his scent now, and there was little chance the sacred ones weren't here to protect this mountain. He gritted his teeth. He was close! Could he really die like this, still a traitor, without telling someone of what he'd found?

He was only halfway across the stone basin when he heard another ear-splitting cry. He froze, turning to find a kerosemal at the top of the basin, its gigantic eyes locked on him. It trumpeted again before it launched itself down the slope in the span of a heartbeat, its spear-like legs making easy work of the stone. He knew how fast a kerosemal could run, and it was far faster than a man. Still, somehow he found a sliver of calm, his father's words coming to him. *Only a welkouyan can find the Mind. It takes all three eyes to see the truth, after all.*

Kishtoran stopped running, standing on the stone and closing his eyes. He could feel the ground shaking from the kerosemal, but he ignored it. He took in a deep breath and let it out slowly, seeing the golden light behind his eyes. He reappeared as a beru hawk, his thick talons on the stone, his powerful wings folded up beside him. The moment the transformation was done, he began to flap, leaving the ground just as the kerosemal reached him. He banked hard to the right as its jaws snapped out, the creature's breath like a furnace even with the sun on him.

He could see the teeth in his periphery, a dull yellow and longer than his arm, but he had no time to consider them further. The kerosemal was absurdly fast, spinning on its ten legs and launching itself at him again. Luckily, his heart had chosen right, the wings of the beru hawk turning him again in a sharp twist, just escaping the next bite. The kerosemal roared in fury, but Kishtoran was already flapping as hard as he could towards the mountain, knowing he wouldn't get lucky a third time.

He went only for speed, not wanting to risk going higher. The kerosemal could likely climb that stone summit faster than a hawk could anyway, and he knew how easily it could catch him in the open air. He could make out a fissure in the stone ahead of him now, though, a gap in the green covered stone that should just fit a man. Were those…trees on the slopes? Kishtoran spared a glance back, finding the kerosemal gaining on him again. He flew in a zigzag pattern, trying to stay free of the jaws and the tail that flailed about like a whip. Just a little longer!

He heard more roars behind him, the rest of the pack finally reaching the basin. Even as a bird, he could feel the ground shaking from the weight of all those awful legs. He pushed his wings past their breaking point, angling up the slope towards that fissure as he pressed on. He could sense the kerosemal just behind him now, but there was no time to look back, no time to dodge. Twenty feet, ten, five; he felt the hot furnace on his back again and put everything into his last push. He. Would. Not. Die. Like. This! He tucked his wings as he reached the end, creating a final burst of speed.

Kishtoran shot into the fissure like an arrow, hitting the

ground at a roll as the kerosemal's jaws slammed into the rock, seeming to shake the entire mountain with its force. It scrambled against the rock, barking as it twisted its head back and forth, trying to lock its eyes on him. Thankfully, the fissure held, too narrow for the huge shoulders of the hunter. Kishtoran pushed himself back onto his talons, glowing again as he regained his human form. His chest was still heaving, but he turned to face the kerosemal and bowed low.

"*Sendorenusaya*," he said loudly in the language of the gods. An image came to his mind of a man bowing before his queen. *I honor you,* it seemed to say. This was the kerosemal's valley after all, the home of the treasure they'd been created to protect. Without them, how could the Mind have stayed secure for so many centuries? But he was no thief; he was here to fulfill the prophesy.

Whether the creature heard the word or simply gave up, it stopped snapping its jaws. It lowered its head onto the ground, closing all of its eyes save the one on the top of its head. It locked this one on to Kishtoran as it breathed deeply in and out.

Kishtoran bowed again before turning deeper into the fissure, unwilling to risk anything more.

He moved slowly through the crack in the stone, staring up at the crags that surrounded him. There was a sliver of sky at the top, if only just, before the crack was covered, turning into a sort of giant tunnel that pushed through the side of the mountain. It was some thirty yards to the other side, and it continued narrowing the whole way. By the end, he was forced to walk sideways, shuffling along the edge of the crack with his chest nearly pressed to the stone. He could hear what sounded like a great wind ahead, the rushing sound pushing its way into the crack from whatever awaited him on the other side.

He finally made it through and stopped in his tracks, blinking in surprise. That was no wind he'd heard, but the rushing of…water. The crack had opened up into a far wider pass, some thirty feet of perfect blue sky looking down on him from above. There was a winding path that climbed deeper into the mountain, but to his left, the entire thing gave way to a yawning trench in the stone, a massive waterfall dropping into the darkness from the center of the mountain. He had never seen so much water! It was like the Snake River, only about a dozen times wider with more water gushing from the rock in a second than his people could drink in a lifetime. There were even more plants there, stubby bushes covered in dark leaves that seemed to grow from every possible crack in the sheer stone.

Kishtoran walked on. If he hadn't believed it from the green alone, this was proof that he had come to the right place. No matter where you were, water was life, but it was all the more so in the depths of the spirit lands. Only the work of Wellonai could have summoned so much to a place so barren.

Before him, to the right of the waterfall, was a giant opening in the center of the mountain, an arch some fifteen feet high where his path ended, disappearing into absolute darkness. What would be waiting for him in there? He pictured the head of the kerosemal. If those fearsome creatures guarded this place, would their goddess take the same form? Or was she more like the humans? The ocean-bound said it was Wellonai's daughter Vilodai that had made the humans, but surely that didn't include the Relimora. Ocean-bound couldn't hear the stones, after all, or at least not anymore…

He shook his head, continuing on the path. If there was ever a time to be awestruck, it was now, but there simply wasn't time. Even if the prophesy was timeless, it wouldn't be long before those poraskuns dug up that palladium. Still, he walked slowly, hugging the wall on his right as he skirted that chasm. He couldn't tell from where he was if it had a bottom, and he wasn't keen to find out.

Finally, he reached the cavern and stood at the edge, squinting into the darkness. It was impossible to tell how deep it was — no way to know how large the mountain was, for that matter — but the floor seemed to be flat at least. As he watched, he finally noticed a silver glow in the darkness. So it wasn't entirely dark, then… He watched the glow for a time, trying to make it out. Whatever it was, it had to be quite large, because it seemed to reach to the cavern's ceiling. As he stared longer, he also noticed a rhythm to the glowing, like a heartbeat, the light growing slightly stronger before dimming to near blackness again.

Kishtoran stepped into the cavern, his fear of pitfalls vanishing as the light pulled him in. The infinite blackness hardly seemed to matter anymore, his eyes focused only on the light as he walked steadily forward. Finally, he reached it, his eyes widening as he took in its source. It was a pillar shaped like a giant gemstone. It was some twenty feet wide, taking up the full height of the cavern and more, its top and bottom disappearing into the stone. In some places it seemed evenly cut, almost like the work of a jeweler, but in others — especially at the top and bottom — it seemed to have grown of its own accord, new lengths of stone burrowing into the rock like the roots of some gigantic tree.

He closed his eyes, basking in the light in front of the stone. He realized now that the gem was humming, a sort of whirring noise that came and went to the pulse of the glows. He opened his eyes again, running them over the length of the structure. In between the pulses of light, he realized there was a steady shimmer behind it. It wasn't just a gem…it was a giant vein of palladium, somehow embedded in the crystal. For a moment, he thought to speak to it, like he would a normal stone, but he didn't dare. Even here, where he may as well admit he had fulfilled the prophecy, he refused to abandon piety. Wellonai had left them the voices for a reason, and it was sacrilege to think she would speak directly to a human, even here.

Still, there were things required of him. Finally remembering himself, he knelt before the crystal and lowered his head, muttering the prayers of the prophecy.

"Your life to our life, oh Wellonai," he said, finding his voice surprisingly shaky. "Your mind to our mind. We have wandered in our disarray, searching eagerly for your fulfillment. For the rebirth of your soul, and the freedom of our spirit, may my lungs be your lungs, my voice be your voice, and my hands be your hands." With that last line, he opened his palms, taking in a wavering breath as he pressed his hands against the pillar and—

His vision was gone, replaced by a vast silvery field. It was almost as if the pulsing glow of the pillar had entered his mind — or he had entered it. He thought to blink, to cry out, to do anything, but he wasn't even sure if he still existed. Just as suddenly, though, he felt the space in his mind expanding. He found he could reach out from that void, albeit only in his mind's eye, but he could see the world through a haze as he did as an esskousel.

He could see out from the form of the crystal pillar, only far, far further than he ever had on his own. It was like seeing the whole world and beyond, a thousand lifetimes of information entering his mind in the span of a heartbeat. He pushed out with all his might, seeing the world as it curved away, the stretch of infinite inky blackness beyond the sky. And there, at the edge of the darkness were stars, and he…knew them somehow, knew in an instant exactly how far away they were and what each one should be called…

He stayed that way for a long while — though time barely seemed to have meaning inside the pillar — soaking in the expanse until a chattering tickled against his awareness. He pulled himself back towards the mountain, staying just wide enough to capture the spirit lands and the swath of Relimora that lay beyond it. He listened to the chattering, trying to pick one voice out of the crowd. They were the voices of…everything. Not just the voices from the stones and the wind he knew so well, but truly *everything*.

The dunes, the oases, all the things that had seemed impossible to speak to seemed to carry a fragment of the Mind of Wellonai. Perhaps they hadn't spoken loudly enough for even a welkouyan like him to hear, but he could sense them now, their voices resonating with the pulse of the pillar. He suddenly thought of the kerosemal. Where were they in all this? As soon as they entered his mind, somehow they were also there in his awareness, their presence pulling at his mind. There were *hundreds* of them patrolling the spirit lands. He picked one in particular at random, and his awareness moved towards it on its own, as easily as moving his finger on a map.

The kerosemal was at an oasis, though one Kishtoran had never seen before, what must be fifty miles to the east of the mountain, deeper into the spirit lands than any human had ever traveled, surely. Its snout was buried in the shaded pool, its jaws working as it gulped the water. Kishtoran felt something of his own presence — or the pillar's rather — in the water, knowing unconsciously that the water must have traveled all that way from the waterfall in Wellonai's mountain. He turned his attention back to the kerosemal and listened to the vibrations of its mind. Without meaning to, he began to vibrate to that rhythm himself, and suddenly, he found himself *inside* the kerosemal, his awareness still reaching out seemingly without limit, but from a smaller vessel.

It seemed he could still hear the voices of the world from the kerosemal, the whispers of life that were abundant even in this place. There were birds crisscrossing the sky up above and sand weevils burrowing below. Even the handful of plants and trees at the oasis had a vibration to them. He watched them for a time as the kerosemal drank, but suddenly, there was a shudder that cut through the silvery light of his vision. It had come somewhere from the south… As Kishtoran put his attention in that direction, he heard a series of shrill cries, like the wailing of a baby, albeit one that carried through this strange awareness. It seemed the kerosemal could sense it too, the creature stopping its drinking to lift its head, focusing all of its eyes on the same point to the south.

Part of him thought to wonder at that — he had always wanted to know how the kerosemal tracked humans across the dunes — but there wasn't time, those horrible cries demanded his attention. As soon as the first one fell away, another followed immediately after. It had come from the same direction, though it seemed even shriller than the first. He needed to get back to the mountain, to see from the wider vantage… With only that thought, it seemed he was back in the pillar, the miles seemingly crossed in the blink of an eye. Convenient that, if he could figure out how to control it better…

Kishtoran reached back out with his mind, stretching his awareness to the south. He wasn't sure where they were until…there! He heard another cry and shifted his presence, reaching it as quickly as he had the kerosemal. There were a great many voices there, all of them ricocheting against his awareness, nearly as overwhelming as the stars had been.

Information began to pour into his mind, but he found he already knew this place, even as strange as it felt to see it from above. This was his home, the Red Land Keep of the Pentine Clan, though not in the state he'd left it… The city was in absolute chaos.

The walls were surrounded by Kikaso archers, their arrows cutting across his vision with a strange light. So they had gotten the palladium out then… The human fragment of himself wanted to curse the poraskuns, but the power of the column was so great that he didn't seem to have room for that kind of feeling in his consciousness anymore. As he watched, an arrow buried itself in one of the western walls, causing another ear-splitting cry as the wall exploded. He tried to hear the mind of the wall, but it seemed the arrows were stealing their voices. Or rather replacing them with a sort of…blankness, the clay that had been formed into the walls by generations of vikousel turning back into nothing but random clumps of dirt, their minds reset to something only the Mind of Wellonai could still sense.

The city's vikousel were all there, trying to rebuild the walls as Pentine archers fired back against the Kikaso, providing scant cover to the lines of spearman rushing to take back the hills surrounding the city. Even as the pillar took away much of his emotion, there was still one person he found his heart yearning for — the Queen, the only person he couldn't bear to fail. Even if the prophesy had been fulfilled, how would he live with himself if she died in this attack? There wasn't time to look for her, though. Another explosion was followed by a sharp cry as the Keros Gate Wall fell, crushing the vikousel who had been trying to shore it up. If the city was fully breached, there was no question what the Kikaso would do to his people, let alone his Queen. They needed their walls back, and they needed them now.

Kishtoran reached out with the Mind of Wellonai, gathering all those tiny minds of clay from the destroyed walls. Surprisingly, they had no memories, as if they'd been wiped clean, the ancient walls suddenly no better than newborns. Still, they latched on to him like kittens to their mother, and he found he could put them back together. He gathered all of the walls up

— the ones that still stood and the ones that had collapsed — and at the same moment, he pulled them all upwards. The earth shook beneath the city as the bedrock got caught up in his pulling, and they soared upwards, the new walls lifting into the air, at least ten times larger than they'd been before.

Arrows continued to pour on the city in volleys, but it seemed that with his hands on the walls, the little nuggets of palladium were no longer enough to break their minds. Still, he couldn't let the Kikaso keep their positions. They'd destroy the walls again the moment he stepped away. He reached out for the hillsides, the mighty stone outcroppings that had surrounded the city for millennia. He expected a delay, a lifetime of waiting on sleepy vitrosen training him to expect no less. Instead, they responded immediately, their minds becoming like putty under the force of Wellonai. He paused, the human part of himself still able to feel some surprise. No-one had ever woken the vitrosen around the Pentine Clan. The stone there was immense, not just a single whale like the ridgeline in the desert, but like the ocean itself.

Wellonai, the stone said, seeming to recognize the power of the pillar in him.

Sekoreinalamay, Kishtoran ordered. The ground began to quake, the hills themselves cleaving at the top, the Kikaso falling away as they were buried under the earth. He found himself feeling an immense sadness as some of them died, their voices snuffed out in an instant, the fragments of light that made up their minds drifting away. The pillar was there to preserve the minds that Wellonai had so carefully poured into the world, but even that was hard to feel under the weight of the pillar's power. How many deaths must it have witnessed before, waiting in the spirit lands as the world unfurled around it? For the briefest moment, he thought he could see that history, flashing through his mind like the memories of the stone, only far more vast.

He shook himself back to the present, forcing himself to release the stones, their quaking finally subsiding. As the earth stilled itself again, there was only silence, and then…cheering. The vikousel threw their fists in the air as the spearman ran up the broken hills to arrest what remained of the Kikaso. It was finished, but there was still one thing he had to do — he had to

find his Queen.

Minara remained in the back of her mind, drifting languidly in the darkness as Minarin directed the troops. After getting the Berillai to the inner fortress, they'd gone directly to the central viewing tower.

She'd always thought the tower to be merely decorative. There were a few ceremonies on it each year, but why have a tower in the center of a city other than to show off? What could you really see that you couldn't from the walls? She'd always been cheeky growing up, but her father had never looked fiercer than when she made fun of the tower — and he'd always been a stern man, regardless of which mind he was speaking with. Even with all the gilded heirlooms in her family, he'd always called the tower the "true treasure" of the Pentine Clan.

How he would have laughed now to see her proven so incredibly wrong. They could see the entire battle from where they were, and she supposed the ancients, with their far more powerful welkouyans, could have done something about the walls even from here. As it stood, though, the battle certainly didn't seem to be going their way and the vantage point didn't help much. The western walls — a far more ancient treasure than this bloody tower — were completely gone, and the Keros Gate didn't look much better.

That's what had sent her to the back of her mind. Now that they were almost surely going to lose, she just wanted a bit of time to herself before the end. Once those poraskuns fully breached the walls, she'd almost certainly be put to the spear. And while Minarin liked to play the fierce warrior when it came to directing troops, it would almost certainly fall on Minara — ever the statesmen — to face death on their behalf.

She pulled herself back to the front of her mind, just behind her eyes so she could watch what Minarin was up to. Sorenin was still by her side — in Kishtoran's form, of course — and Minarin was talking with the Spearmaster as they pointed at the columns of spears who were futilely trying to take the hills under the fire of those strange arrows. Her vikousel seemed to think they were fragments of palladium, doing something to ruin the minds of the walls. She hoped they'd be able to rebuild them, but they hadn't seemed to have much luck yet, and what was to stop those arrows from ruining the new walls, too? At least the poraskuns seemed to be slowing their volleys. They were still firing plenty of normal arrows, of course, but the palladium ones seemed to be growing less frequent. Or maybe there were just fewer walls to hit… At any rate, the new arrows made a strange whistling sound as they cut through the air, so at least they knew when one was coming.

Just then, another shrill whistle tore through the air from the western hills. Minarin stopped mid-sentence, their eyes darting across the sky as she tried to spot it. The moment they locked on to it, however, the arrow buried itself into what remained of the Keros Gate, causing a massive explosion. Even from afar on the tower, they were thrown from their feet. Their minds were scrambled for a moment, and Minara felt herself scrambling against the stone, desperately trying to keep from going over the edge. Somehow, Sorenin was there, picking her up by the elbow.

"Perhaps we should flee, my lady?" he asked.

"No," Minarin said, regaining control, "we stay until the

end." She looked to the Spearmaster, who simply nodded.

Minarin took them back to the edge of the tower. As they were squinting through the smoke, however, the ground began to shake.

"What in the Mother's name is that?" Minarin asked, looking around them. Sorenin came up behind them, grabbing them by the shoulder and pulling them away from the edge as the ground seemed to bounce around them. A great cracking sound came from the edge of the city and dust began to fly in all directions. They all fell over again, clinging to the tower as it shook like a mero tree in the wind. Minarin closed their eyes tightly, fear flooding their mind. Perhaps this was the end after all — not a sword, but a fall from the tower, their body crumpled into nothing as the earth itself gave up on them.

Just as soon as it began, though, the quaking stopped. And then, in the utter silence that followed, there was…cheering. Her heart skipped a beat again, but the cheering sounded close, far too close to be the cheers of those poraskuns destroying their city. Minarin pushed them to their feet, their eyes darting again as they found the city's walls were whole. Not only whole, they were…gigantic. Could this mean…the…prophesy?

They were turning towards the others, searching for an answer, when there was a loud buzzing sound. For a moment, she feared another attack, but the air itself seemed to shine, a silvery glow surrounding them until suddenly, Kishtoran was there. Or not Kishtoran himself…more like a copy, like the silvery ghosts they said wandered Seruva at night. He stood in the center of the tower, Sorenin's version of him still visible, standing agape just behind him. The phantom Kishtoran's eyes were locked on hers, and he opened his mouth, his voice carrying through all the chaos below, like his voice was *inside* her mind.

"The prophesy has been fulfilled," he said. "My Queen, my…love, I'm so sorry. I brought this attack upon you, but… It is done!"

Without thinking, Minarin surrounded them with golden light, pulling their forms apart as she ran to Kishtoran, throwing her arms around the silvery figure. Minara stood there, her mouth hanging open, her eyes darting around the tower as the other guards stared back. They had never been apart in front of so many eyes. It was…unprecedented, maybe even a sacrilege. No-one but the direct servants of the royal family knew of the twin esskousel who had always ruled the Pentine Clan. Sorenin knew, of course, from his mother's service, but he looked equally horrified.

But then, Minara laughed. The laughter bubbled out of her on its own accord, shaking her stomach until tears came to her eyes. She fell to her knees, wracked by laughter until she moved towards the edge of the tower, letting her legs dangle over the edge as she looked out at the new walls of her city. The prophesy had been *fulfilled*. It didn't matter who ruled the clan anymore. Let Minarin rule alongside Kishtoran, for all she cared. All the careful diplomacy, all the training, all of it was nothing compared to that. Her favorite line of the prophesy floated up to her: "When the ground quakes, and the barriers of men are no more, there shall be no kings, only the freedom of our gods to walk again, to dwell in the spirit and walk among the stars."

She was free. And more importantly, so were her people.

After millennia in this desert, awaiting this day, it had somehow

arrived when no-one expected it. It had been done. They were all

free.

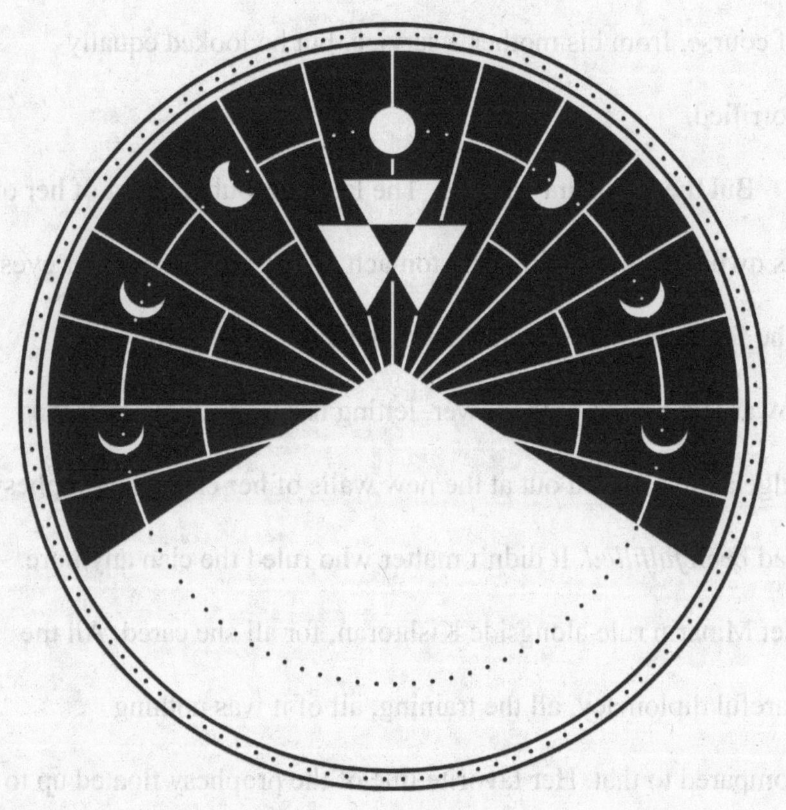